WINDSOR PA[ST]

REMINISCE

BY PAUL JOHNSON

Laughing at the Past

outskirts
press

Outskirts Press, Inc.
http://www.outskirtspress.com

ISBN: 978-1-9772-5400-9

Outskirts Press and the "OP" logo are trademarks belonging to Outskirts Press, Inc.

PRINTED IN THE UNITED STATES OF AMERICA

ACKNOWLEDGEMENTS

Like to dedicate this book to my family and friends.
Also, thanks to the Windsor Park Boys. Without them,
I couldn't have put our fictional story together (wink, wink).

Special thanks to my wife, who encourages
me to keep writing and cartooning.

.

CONTENTS

INTRODUCTION

These are the stories about the Windsor Park Boys growing up in the fifties, sixties, and seventies. Some of the stories came from various sources, but most came from the leftover minds of the Windsor Park Boys, whose names had to be changed to protect the guilty.

Ever keep in touch with the friends you grew up with? Reminiscing about the things you did as kids. Going to grade school, hanging out after school, getting your first car. How about going to high school? Remember when you started to date? I know it wasn't always fun times. Sometimes they were downright embarrassing. Sometimes they were hilarious. Reminiscing is not only fun, but it can be therapeutic. Life was different growing up in the '50s, '60s, and '70s. Every household didn't have a computer, or an iPad. No one was texting each other on smartphones. If we wanted to see or talk to someone we would meet at a certain spot or go over to their house. We were outside guys that entertained ourselves. Not saying we were the smartest kids in the school, but we own up to what we did as kids, because it happened. We survived growing up. We like to look on the funny side of life. Life is too short not to laugh.

My name is Henry Perkins, and Larry Collins and I are going to narrate to you some stories about our growing up with the Windsor Park Boys. Hopefully our stories will get you to reminisce about your childhood friends and the funny things that you went through. Some parts of our stories may not be suitable for your visual enjoyment, and Larry might use some language for adults only.

Larry had two sisters, and I had two sisters and two brothers. Larry and I hung out all the time even though we had opposite personalities. Larry was a thick-headed child who turned into a rock-and-roll risk-taker and is now stuck in the sixties and seventies.

Larry and I lived behind each other.

"Don't remind me, Henry. Like those ranch houses in Windsor Park were so close, my sisters could see you in the bathroom getting ready for school. They told me you totally stayed way too long in front of the mirror. Just like a girl."

"Larry, please, let's start at the beginning of the story."

Windsor Park was a neighborhood built in the fifties near the Crompton Textile Mills in West Warwick, Rhode Island. I was only four years old when my parents moved us there. Memories of all the fun times still race through my head. Kids growing up together not realizing that one day we'd grow apart. It was there we were forever molded into the Windsor Park Boys.

Windsor Park was home to a lot of families. The kids in the families ranged from teenagers on down. We all had different descents: Irish, Swedish, Polish, French-Canadian, Italian, Scottish, and Indian. All-American mixed-breed boys. Larry, I'll never forget meeting you for the first time. We were only four years old. I was standing in the corner puddle across the street from my house when you rode over on your tricycle. It was such an innocent time.

CATHOLIC SCHOOL

CLASS, HENRY AND LARRY ARE HERE TO REMINISCE FOR THE DAY.

M ost of the Windsor Park Boys went to Catholic schools. Everyone in school had to wear uniforms. One day my classmate came in with a brand-new shirt, not even washed yet. Unknown to everyone, if you perspired, the chemicals they used in the shirt made it smell really bad. Well he wore the shirt all week and earned the nickname "Stinky." Everyone teased him including myself. I didn't realize why he smelled until my parents bought me a new shirt and I wore it to school. I felt Stinky's pain. I thought it was the worst day of my life. I happened to get the shirt real dirty that day and my mom had to wash it. Then I noticed the shirt didn't smell anymore. I am still traumatized to this day and wash everything new before I wear it.

The Catholic schools were taught by nuns. I remember the nuns making us feel comfortable when we first started at Saint Mary's School. It wasn't until the fifth grade, when we had Sister Agnes, God rest her soul, that the comfortable feeling went away.

The little black-and-white pit bull taught respect the old-fashioned way. She was hands-on, right in your face, straightened you out right away. She never held back and always said what went through her mind. No filter included with this nun. There was nothing graceful about her either.

"Larry, remember when Sister Agnes left the classroom and you started crawling up and down the classroom aisles on your knees, until you noticed black nun shoes in front of you?"

During chorus she would pace up and down in front of everyone, listening for someone off-key. I swear she could hear a bug fart. She picked me right out of the whole chorus and basically told me to be quiet. So, for the rest of the year I just moved my mouth faking it. There went my singing career.

All the nuns had large wooden clickers. A barrel-like cylinder attached to a six-inch handle. They were made of oak and walnut with brass wire or rubber bands to activate the clicker. One click, we would have to stand. Two clicks, we would start to walk. One loud whop and you knew someone got Sister Agnes pissed off. You never knew when it was coming. One click, and one had to obey. Before any holy event, we'd have clicker training. We were taught when to walk, sit, kneel, stand up, and genuflect all by the number of clicks. The nuns carried the clickers around their waist. Sister Agnes walked around like a cop on a beat with a nightstick. I remember Mother Superior telling Sister Agnes not to use her old (Mafia)–style discipline on us. Sister Agnes replied, "Well it works." I knew we were in trouble after that remark. I should say Larry was in big trouble because he was the only one that acted up in fifth grade. Everyone else was too afraid of Sister Agnes.

The nuns wanted to make money for a fundraiser. Sister Agnes had a great idea: buy a dozen donuts and sell them individually during lunchtime. Larry and I were chosen to sell the donuts. So, before lunch, we walked to the donut shop to buy the donuts. On the way back, Larry (a couple of sandwiches short of a picnic) decided to play football with the box of donuts and passed the box to me. Of course, the box opened and the donuts fell all over the sidewalk. We quickly brushed them off, put them back into the box, and off we went. Because it was our opening day we sold all the donuts. Later, one younger kid came up to our donut table and said, "I found a rock in my donut." I looked at Larry, and with a *cat that ate the canary* smile, Larry said, "There's no charge for the rock." We didn't sell too many more rock-flavored donuts after that. The nuns never did figure out why the donut fundraiser never made it.

The first time I heard the F-bomb was in Catholic school. Martha Kelly dropped it one day after lunch. She was trying to act big in front of her friends. I decided to try it out myself in front of my friends. I said, "What the F-bomb is going on, guys?"

"Henry, I never laughed so hard watching the expression on Martha Kelly's face when you said that."

"I couldn't believe it either, Larry." She started bitch-slapping the hell out of me. I said, "What the hell was that for, you crazy bitch!" Then she slapped me some more. I said, "I just heard you say the F-bomb!" Martha's remark was, "But you're Henry Perkins, that should never had come out of your mouth."

The nuns would march us up to Saint Mary's Church for May Procession practice. The May Procession was a special ceremony to Mary, Mother of Jesus. We would walk about a mile from the school to the church. About halfway there, I told Sister Agnes I had to go to the bathroom. Her reply was, "You should have gone before we left school." I deemed her the Sister of NO Mercy after that.

Talk about going to church and sitting in your own pew! I just couldn't hold it anymore. The smell wreaked havoc. Everyone was blaming the person beside them. So, to cover my tracks, I started pointing to the person beside me. I think they figured it out because, well let's just say nobody walked home with me after practice. "Saint Mary's Church, built in 1844 and christened in 1962, row twelve, seat three."

Our eighth-grade teacher Sister Josephine was the biggest nun you ever saw. She was six foot three and two hundred pounds. She could be very intimidating and convincing when she walked and talked. We had just learned the biblical story about young David defeating the Philistine giant Goliath, in single combat, with a slingshot and a rock. During recess, while playing baseball, Larry, with a bat and hard rubber ball, hit a line drive off the head of the giant nun. Her glasses flew about twenty feet from her face. She rolled to the left and rocked to the right. Just when we thought she was going down, she caught herself, shook her head, then shook her fist and said with a smile, "I'll get even for this."

Well that afternoon Sister Josephine told all the boys who were playing baseball to line up in the hallway with their sleeves rolled up. She said we were all getting an important shot from the doctor. Of course, there was no doctor or shot. I can still hear her laughing and saying, "Payback!"

"I must admit, Henry. She was a good giant nun, but a large target. I remember hitting Mother Superior during recess about two weeks later. I swear to God, Henry, I wasn't trying to hit anyone."

"Larry, I bet you wished you accidently hit Sister Agnes for some payback!"

"Man, like that would have really got her nunderpants in a knot!"

Our class belonged to the Saint Dominic Savio Club. Dominic Savio was an Italian student of Saint John Bosco. Dominic was studying to become a priest but died at the age of fourteen. He was noted for his piety and devotion to the Catholic faith and eventually became a saint. The club is an association of young people who desire to follow the example of the boy saint Dominic Savio. Larry was always nominating me to be the president of the club. The class was always in favor because they thought I was priest material. Larry got the biggest kick watching my face when I was approved. One weekend the boys in the class were sent on a St. Dominic Savio retreat. At the retreat we went to Mass, listened to the Brothers talk about the boy saint, read scriptures, prayed the rosary, and eventually were told to go to our rooms for meditation and contemplation. We had just gotten to our rooms when I heard a knock on my door. I thought it was one of the Brothers. When I opened the door, there was Larry kneeling with his hands folded in a praying position smiling his head off. I laughed and said, "Praying at my door won't bring up our friendship status any higher, but whatever you did I forgive you." Then I asked him what the hell he was doing. A Brother yelled from the end of the hallway, saying he'd caught Larry running around the hallway when we were all told to be in our rooms. I thought we were in fifth grade with Sister Agnes all over again. The Brother insisted I ignore Larry and just shut the door. I laughed and waved my hand good-bye as Larry smiled and shrugged his shoulders.

"Yeah, Henry, I had to kneel and pray at your door for about a half hour."

Father Bulldog was our parish priest. During the Christmas holiday he came to the school to get money trees that the nuns had us make for him. We'd fold the money into flowers or hearts and fastened it to a small artificial tree. It seemed to make him pretty happy.

We nicknamed him Father Bulldog because he was short, had a face like a bulldog and a temperament to match. I always wondered if God made him that way to scare people. He was always yelling at the parishioners during the sermon at Sunday Mass, telling them they weren't giving enough money for the Sunday collections. As young kids we were terrified of him.

Once, when our family missed a Sunday Mass due to unforeseen circumstances, I had the pleasure of being the third family member to explain to him in the confessional about the mortal sin. He was tired of hearing the story and Father went off like a rocket. I think everyone in the church heard him yelling and giving me my penance of ten Hail Marys and ten Our Fathers. Everyone was staring at me as I walked out of the confessional. They must have been wondering what the hell I said in there to get Father Bulldog so upset. Everyone still waiting in line for confession looked scared to death!

"Like, Henry, remember the day I went to confession with Father Bulldog. When he opened up the confessional window, I got so nervous I couldn't remember any of my sins. He said, 'So, you're without sin now.' I started to laugh, then I spurted out, 'I committed adultery.' You should have seen the look on his face. Not sure if impure thoughts are the same as adultery, but it sounded much cooler. He then asked me if I masturbated. So, I answered him with a question: 'Do you?'

"After that confession, every time I bumped into Father Bulldog, he looked at me like I was some kind of a thirteen-year-old sex maniac."

The nuns prepared us to be altar boys. We had to learn a little Latin for the responses during the Mass. We were needed at Sunday Mass, weddings, funerals, and of course during Holy Week.

Larry put Holy Thursday into the altar-boy record books. The church just put new rugs on the altar. "Remember, Larry?"

"I don't recall, Henry."

The incense censer, also called a thurible, was used in processions and important Masses. It is a metal container about the size and shape of a coffeepot suspended on chains. The altar boy lights the charcoal in the censer before he gets on the altar, and during the Mass the priest puts incense in the censer on top of the charcoal. The symbolic value of the smoke is that of sanctification and purification.

After Father walked around the altar with the hot and smoking censer he gave it back to Larry, who accidently opened and dumped its entire contents onto the altar rug. Larry sanctified and purified the new rug. Father Bulldog's eyes almost popped out of his head. He said, "Jesus Christ help us." It must have looked kind of funny from the congregation's view. Father yelling at us to get some water. Larry, almost pouring the communion water on it until Father told us to get tap water from the sanctuary. We poured water on the burning rug, which made more smoke. The altar boys were all smiling until Father gave us his mean bulldog look.

Occasionally Larry and I would be the altar boys during the Stations of the Cross. This is a service commemorating Jesus Christ's last day on earth as a man. We carried lit candles and stood on either side of the priest at each station. There are fourteen stations. Father Bulldog, having problems breathing because of his addiction to cigarettes, would breathe heavily after talking at each station. He kept blowing out our candles. One parishioner took out a match and lit the candles for us, but he'd blow them out again. We both felt kind of weird carrying unlit candles around for an hour.

The memory that stuck out the most being an altar boy was this girl's neck. You see, in the sixties the altar boy during Holy Communion would carry a plate with a handle, called a communion plate. During communion the altar boy put it under the chin of the person getting communion, so the host wouldn't fall on the floor in case of a mishap. The altar had a small railing in the front, and during communion the parishioners would kneel around it. The priest would start at one end of the railing and then walk back to the beginning. One Mass I was behind Father Bulldog walking back to the beginning of the communion line carrying my communion plate, not realizing a girl had her neck stretched way over the railing.

Not being able to see her because of Father's robe flying around, I clobbered her right in the face with the plate. When we came to her to give her Holy Communion, she was red-faced, glossy-eyed, and a little skittish of the altar boy with the plate. I felt bad I hit her, even though she had her neck stretched over the railing. Believe it or not, at the next Sunday Mass I was walking behind the priest and I almost hit giraffe girl right in the face—again! By the time we got to her, I had visions of smacking her on top of her head for being stupid.

AFTER SCHOOL

After school was a fun time. We did all sorts of things that kept us busy. One thing we did was to have grape fights. Windsor Park was surrounded by wild grapes hanging from the trees. You could smell the aroma all through the plat. While heading into the woods to do battle, we met Rider filling up his little red wagon with piles of grapes for ammunition.

Rider was the only child of Polish and Italian parents. He lived a couple of blocks away from Larry and me. His last name was hard to pronounce, so someone nicknamed him Rider and it stuck. He was the quietest and nicest Windsor Park Boy that Larry had the pleasure of corrupting.

We met some older Windsor Park Boys in the woods and the war started. To beat the older Windsor Park Boys, it meant we'd have to outsmart them by using guerrilla warfare. So Rider, my brother Mike, Larry, and I went in the trees and on the ground crawling around in some green and reddish leafy vines. We were ambushing and splattering grapes over everyone. Tardy, one of the older Windsor Park Boys, asked us if we knew what we were crawling around in. We didn't know what he was talking about—until the next day. That was the first time we learned about poison ivy. "Do you remember that day, Larry?"

"Oh yeah, I can tell yah, I had poison ivy in unmentionable places. I still remember the calamine lotion baths. The Grape War came to an unforgettable and itchy end."

We met Little Z and Big Z when they walked my brother home after he was bitten by a dog while riding his bike around the block.

The Z Brothers were friends of Rider and lived about a block from him. They're our Polish Windsor Park brothers. Their last name sounded like it began with a Z. Thus was the beginning of their nicknames. We all enjoyed having pea-shooting battles. Buy a box of peas from Koch's Store, get a straw at home, and off to battle you go. With a mouthful of peas, you could get those peas coming out of that straw like a machine gun.

It was fun until you swallowed a pea or two. We were in my parents' backyard when a couple of peas accidently hit some kids in the neighboring yard. An argument erupted and the words and peas started flying. I called a truce and lured them close to our six-foot picket fence. We had my dad's water hose turned on ready to blast them. My mom was watching everything and started yelling, "What are you kids up to? You leave them alone!"

"What a bummer, Henry. Talk about missed opportunities in life."

Windsor Park had a bunch of brothers that were close in age. Brothers that close always seem to argue and fight. One set was our Irish Windsor Park Boys. One day while sitting on a lawn in Windsor Park, the brothers started fighting. A bunch of us were watching them bitch-slapping each other, rolling around on the ground, threatening to tell their mother on each other.

Big Z said, "There goes the Smackum Brothers." From then on, we called them Little and Big Smackum.

Mr. Jenkins was the grumpy old guy in the neighborhood. He didn't like the Windsor Park Boys. He wasn't prejudiced, he just hated everyone, especially us. The Smackum Brothers' family lived right next to him. Their father had a long-standing feud with Mr. Jenkins and it started to boil over. Jenkins' tree branches hung over the Smackums' fence. I remember the Smackums' dad telling all of us that he'd called a lawyer to find out if he could cut Mr. Jenkins' tree branches on his side of the fence. Lawyer said, any branches hanging over the property line were fair game. Smackums' dad grabbed a branch cutter, and with a smile said, "Watch this." As Mr. Jenkins watched, Smackums' dad hacked off his branches all the way down the fence line. Mr. Jenkins was taking a fit. As kids, we thought well this is what happens if you're a meany.

A lot of Windsor Park parents let their kids sleep out in tents. One night my brother Mike and I slept out in our parents' backyard. From what the Smackum brothers told us, Mr. Jenkins was still giving their dad problems. The Windsor Park Boys decided to back him up and give Mr. Jenkins a visit around three in the morning. We knew he grew a vegetable garden. So, our mission was to blow up whatever we could and run. We grabbed our salutes, jumped our fence, and headed up to our mark. We packed our explosives all around his tomato and pepper plants, lit the fuses, and ran. Little and Big Smackum were sleeping out in their tent and heard someone running in their backyard. They opened the flap of the tent and waved us in. We were all laughing as I explained our successful mission. When Mr. Jenkins' back light went on, it was time to get back to base before someone noticed us. We looked at it as a little late-night raid on the enemy, to help the Smackums' cause.

Halloween was the payback season. We would steal Jenkins's pumpkin every year just to let him know we could. One year the pumpkin on his stairs had a string tied to it. The string went into the bushes and up into a window. When we picked up the pumpkin, we heard a bell, so we put it back down. He came to the door but we all hid.

Once we found out it was attached to a bell, the fun began. Five of us walked up to his front door, blocking his view, yelling, "Trick or treat!" While waiting for him to get the candy, a sixth Windsor Park Boy cut the line, wrapped the line around the bush, kicked the pumpkin down the stairs to another Windsor Park Boy, who kicked it into the darkness to another Windsor Park Boy, who ran down the street with it. One night Larry had dog poop in a paper bag, put it on his steps, set fire to it, rang the doorbell, then watched Mr. Jenkins stomp in poop. "Sorry, visual discretion advised!"

We tried our skills at building things from the wood we found around town. One day we built a square boat, but it sank in the Pawtuxet River on its maiden voyage. I still have pictures of the wooden go-cart we made with doll carriage wheels. We are sitting in it with football helmets on our heads. Of course, most of the Windsor Park Boys built a fort in their parents' backyard.

I think everyone can remember a steep hill they went down with a sled, go-cart, or bike. Our hill was School Street. This street was not only the steepest hill around, but it also had lumps and holes all the way down. We didn't have the gonads to take the go-cart to the top of the hill. I do remember Big Z going down School Street with his bike, while Rider was sitting side-saddle on the main frame.

"Yeah, Henry, I thought they were screaming like little girls because of the adrenalin rush. It wasn't until they were about forty feet from busy Main Street, flying by us doing about twenty miles per hour, when I heard them screaming, 'Look out! No brakes!' Rider said he gripped the handlebars so tight, Big Z couldn't turn the bike. They flew across both lanes of traffic on Main Street, smashing into the curb."

Big Z went right over Rider and the handlebars. Lucky thing they landed on the library lawn. The town took care of that lawn and it was like landing on a mattress. The bike's front tire and rim had an indentation of the curb, and the fork of the bike was bent back to the frame. I think the only thing stopping them from dropping a biscuit in their pants on School Street that day was the lucky horseshoe they had up their butts.

I'm not sure if we raided his orchard for the apples, the thrill, or both. His apples tasted so good! The first thing we did was to wait till it got dark out. Then we'd make sure the streetlight next to his orchard didn't work. Then we'd jump his fence and grab some apples. We kept taking and eating his apples until he noticed them disappearing. At first, he started yelling at us from his window, telling us his apples were just sprayed with pesticide. When we kept taking them, the apple guy started nightly surveillance missions. He tried everything to catch us. One night he tried to trick us by climbing into one of his apple trees, but we busted him because he picked a night with a full moon. We could see his silhouette in the tree.

Big Z started to bust his balls. "Who's that in the apple tree? Why it's the little old apple guy!" He got pissed like a junkyard dog that got stung by a hornet. By the time he jumped out of that tree, we were halfway down the street.

The next weekend five of the Windsor Park Boys went back for more apples. We raided his orchard so much that I think we schooled him how to catch us. We didn't see him but he was there waiting for us. He was wearing dark clothing and hid in the shadows. When we started grabbing his apples he surprised us. He grabbed my brother's coat but couldn't hold on. My brother barely got away. Mad Mike realized that we were about to get caught. He panicked and nailed the apple guy with a hail of apples to his chest. I'm not sure who was more shocked—the apple guy or us. Apple guy transformed into that junkyard dog and started chasing us through the neighborhood. For a while he was right on our tails. We knew he didn't have the endurance to keep it up. We also knew he wouldn't give up either.

I remember running through a construction site in the pitch-dark, smashing into a pile of lumber and hurting my leg. "Remember, Larry, you picked me up and started running with me over your shoulder."

"Far out, now I remember why my shoulder is killing me. Remind me to sue your sorry butt after the story."

He must have chased us four blocks, yelling and screaming like an Indian on the war path. There was this adrenaline rush that would come over us as we sprinted down the road. It felt like our feet weren't even touching the ground. Being only thirteen years old we could run for miles. When we ran by a streetlight we'd turn around to catch a glimpse of the apple guy. We didn't want to run home to show him where we lived, so we ran into a field and hid. The apple guy must have seen us go in there. He cornered us against a six-foot fence that had bushes and trees in front of it. As long as we didn't move, he couldn't see us. It was so dark out he never knew who was taking his apples. We were always one step ahead of him. Days earlier he saw Little Z at the neighborhood store and blamed him for stealing his apples. Little Z told him he had the wrong guy. (It was actually his brother Big Z who ran with our raiding party.)

He scanned his flashlight ever so slowly along the fence.

It felt like we were trying to escape from a prison. When he scanned the flashlight beam towards the other side of the fence, we made a break for it. Everyone made it over the picket fence except me because of my banged-up leg. Larry grabbed me by the arms and yanked me over.

"Thanks, Larry, I'm not sure where I'd be without my partner in crime."

One bright sunny day Larry and I were walking to the candy store. We bumped into Little Smackum. He was carrying his coat and his face and clothes were covered in soot.

We asked him, "What the hell happened to you?" He said he and a schoolmate were sitting on the grassy hill, which was a beautiful spot overlooking the textile mills and Pawtuxet River. Everyone stopped there after the candy store to eat candy, drink soda, and try out cigarettes. He and a schoolmate were playing with matches, watching the grass burn. Then they would stomp the fire out at the last moment.

Because it was a windy day and the grass was dry, they accidently/on purpose set the grassy hill on fire. They tried to put it out with their coats. Thinking the fire was out and knowing that all the smoke would attract attention, they hightailed it out of there. It must have started back up again. We could hear the fire trucks in the distance. Someone must have pulled the fire alarm because the firemen came pretty quick. We avoided going to the candy store that day. We didn't want to get blamed for that mess. The grassy hill was only blackened in a small area and it eventually became our spot in the sun again. Just not for starting fires.

"Larry, remember the day when a bunch of us were standing outside the local pizza parlor? Someone told you this pizza place had unbreakable front windows. They said you could throw a rock at it and it would bounce back."

"I picked up a rock and threw it at the window. Of course, it went right through the window into the pizza parlor."

The wintertime was great for competitive snowball throwing. The Windsor Park Games had begun. My older brother, Mad Mike, and I were trying to hit telephone poles. Then we noticed a girl walking three telephone poles down. Walking target three poles away. That would win the competition. My brother's first snowball got her right off the head.

It also got her father at our house in record time. We got punished for that feat of accuracy. Hey, being thirteen years old, we thought girls made good targets. We had a lot to learn about girls.

I remember the first time we ever threw a snowball at a car. We were hiding in the woods on that snowy night. The Windsor Park Boys were waiting for that steel prey to drive by. All of a sudden, our first victims' headlights appeared out of the snowflakes. He was traveling really slowly down the hill into our ambush. Then, barrages of snowballs were unleashed from the darkness of the woods. We didn't realize the car window was down until we saw the driver take one in the face. He jammed his brakes on, got out of the car, and chased us through the woods swearing the whole time. I learned a couple of new swear words that night. Boy was he pissed. Lucky for him the snow barely made a good snowball. Lucky for us he never caught us. We were young and stupid.

My younger brother TJ liked competitive snow-throwing too. He decided to make the mother of all snowballs and hum it over an embankment at a passing car. Not thinking of consequences seems to run in the Windsor Park Boys' DNA. Anyways, the rather large meteorite snowball hit the windshield of a passing car. The occupants chased him through the mill parking lot. TJ didn't hang around and ran for his life. What TJ didn't realize, it was our sister and her boyfriend who were chasing him. My sister recognized TJ and decided that she would meet him at home and give him the bad news. The meteorite-snowball-throwing contest would be coming to an end.

EARLY MONEY

'll never forget the first time I enjoyed money—well almost. I was walking by my next-door neighbors' house when I saw a ten-dollar bill blowing around. It was a very windy day, so it could have come from anywhere. Figuring there might be more, I scoured my neighborhood street. There was a five-dollar bill in the gutter in front of my parents' house, and across the street on our neighbors' front lawn was a twenty-dollar bill. I was rich! There wasn't anyone in the area looking to claim my money. As far as I was concerned, it was finders keepers, losers weepers. I couldn't wait to tell my mom of my good fortune. As I was jumping for joy telling Mom how I was going to spend the money, she said, "I hate to be the bearer of bad news." Apparently, a neighbor two houses up called and asked her to be on the lookout for a bunch of money that blew out of her hand. I tried to explain finders keepers, losers weepers to my mom, but she said it doesn't apply in this situation. My first encounter with a lot of money might have only felt good for a while, but that experience sparked something in me.

Even though we were too young to work, we wanted income. Empty soda bottles were two cents for twelve-ounce bottles and five cents for the quart bottles. We had a couple of ways of collecting them. Go walking by the textile mill and make fun of the workers in the windows, so they would throw bottles at us. Scout for them along the side of the road or go door to door through Windsor Park telling everyone we were collecting bottles for the Boy Scouts. The Boy Scout story was a little safer. So, we'd pull our wagon through Windsor Park asking people for bottles. Most people didn't say anything and just gave us their extra bottles. One woman reminded us that the Boy Scouts only collected newspapers. We were snot-nosed kids. The guilt only lasted five seconds.

"Yeah man, then off to the candy store to cash them in."

Later on, we started to work for the local florist. He had a couple of gladiola fields. We would plant the bulbs in the spring, eventually weed the fields, pick the flowers during the summer, and then pull the bulbs in the fall. It paid seventy-five cents an hour. The florist would let this one nutty guy drive one of the two vans that brought us to the fields. Every trip we'd hear, "brake test," and we'd have to hold on for dear life. The driver would slam on the brakes, and anyone who didn't have a handhold would become airborne until a part of him contacted the truck again. The new guys learned really quick. Nut job would also scare the bejesus out of road walkers by slowly coasting alongside them and making the truck backfire. The gladiola trucks had large water coolers in them for the workers in the fields. On the way home, the driver looked for road walkers, slowed the truck to a crawl, then told us to open the back doors and empty the cooler on them.

When weeding around the plants, the florist told everyone he wanted our faces three inches off the ground. Talk about eating a little dirt.

"Cool, man, I remember eating that dirt."

"Larry, you started eating dirt when you were two years old."

When it was flower-cutting season, we rode to the fields sitting on top of crates of Mason jars full of water. The driver would always look for bumps or potholes, making the water splash up to get our backsides soaking wet.

Flower-cutting season was the best time. There was a cutter and a holder. One guy would cut the flowers and pass them back to a holder. When the holder had a dozen, he would tell the cutter. The cutter, who had string around his belt, would tie a dozen gladiola in two spots.

The dozen would be leaned against the rows for pickup. After the cutting was complete, we would throw about ten bundles of flowers over our shoulders, run them to the trucks, and put them in large jars of water which were in wooden cases. Once in a while you could get a free dozen from the florist when you told him your mother or another family member was having a birthday, anniversary, etc. One time, Larry forgot he'd already told the florist his mother was having a birthday. The florist asked him if he had multiple mothers. Of course, Larry lied and told him a story about his two mothers.

PELLET GUN MANIA

We only had a choice of three television channels, but they supplied nonstop military shows like *Hogan's Heroes*, *Rat Patrol*, *Twelve O'clock High*, and *Combat*. Remember the western shows, *Cheyenne* with Clint Walker, *Gunsmoke* with James Arness, *Maverick* with James Garner, *Wanted Dead or Alive* with Steve McQueen, and *Daniel Boone* with Fess Parker? Watching all these shows on television made us interested in getting BB guns.

"Yeah, Henry, like the shows were loud and intense. I couldn't wait to shoot at something to be just like them."

I remember getting my first gun, a Daisy BB rifle. Can't say it was too powerful. My older brother Mad Mike and I would come home from school and shoot birds in the backyard. Of course, we'd make sure no one was around. One day before I got home from school, Mike said he shot six birds and put them in our trash barrel. Being competitive I went to the trash barrel to count them. Well, when I took the cover off the trash barrel, all of them flew out. Apparently, they were only knocked out.

Eventually we bought pellet rifles with scopes on them. One day, when I came home from school, I noticed a blackbird in our backyard maple tree. I opened the window just enough to stick the barrel of the rifle out. I looked over our six-foot picket fence and saw my next-door neighbor watering his lawn. I knew I could make the shot before he'd see anything. When I hit the bird, it hung upside down and started making a loud squawking sound. The neighbor walked over to the fence with his eyes in disbelief, only to watch the bird fall to the ground.

I started to panic, but was hoping he thought it had a heart attack. I guess we all know that only happens when they land on live electrical wires. After he walked into his house, our phone started ringing.

I knew I was in trouble so I didn't dare answer it. Thank God no one was home and he never called back.

I told my brother we had to cool it for a week or so. After the cooling-off period, I opened the window to check the bird situation and noticed that my neighbor's window had a hole in it. Machinegun Mike ended the backyard hunting grounds. Windsor Park had plenty of woods around it. So, we decided to graduate into the woods. Most of the Windsor Park Boys grew up with pellet guns. It was a kid thing in the sixties.

As we got older we became sensitive about shooting birds. Remember when Rider shot that robin? The one his neighbor Mrs. Heeding used to feed out of her hand? In Rider's defense we were young and immature. I remember like it was yesterday. He walked over to Mrs. Heeding's house with that dead robin behind his back. Being ashamed and not knowing what to say, he showed the dead robin to her and with a tear in his eye said, "I think this belongs to you." That poor lady screamed for hours. She gave it a beautiful burial. I hear she's at the local nursing home. We should visit her.

THE ROCKS

Spending a lot of time in the woods hunting eventually took us to the Rocks. The Rocks were part of an old stone wall bordering a body of water called the Trench. The Trench was dug as a waterway to channel water from the Pawtuxet River to a pumphouse that used water to turn machinery inside the mills. The Rocks were about seventy-five yards from the mill. They fronted on the Trench and were camouflaged by trees and brush to the extent that no one could see you when you were there. It was a bunch of rocks where teenagers could sit and socialize. A spot where we could all meet and get away from grown-ups. We'd eat, drink, talk, and have a nice fire. This was a special place where the Windsor Park Boys could be themselves.

It was at the Rocks on July 3, 1967 that we drank our first beer.

Cochise's house was close to the Rocks, so we all asked our parents if we could sleep out in tents behind his house. Cochise was given his nickname when his father told us one of his ancestors came from an Indian tribe. Our Indian Windsor Park Boy Cochise was full of mischief and loved being in the woods.

Once we all had permission to sleep out, we hid a few cases of beer and a bottle of hard stuff to get ready for the night. Then, as it got dark, we snuck over to the Rocks and began to drink. Our older Italian Windsor Park Boy who we called Elvis slept out too. He wore his clothes and hair like Elvis. So, we nicknamed him Elvis.

Elvis drank the hard stuff; the rest of the Windsor Park Boys drank Colt 45 and Budweiser beer. Larry drank too much and couldn't make it back to Cochise's house. So, we dragged him back to the tent by his feet. We were laughing so loud Cochise's father figured out what we were up to.

He drove his car into the backyard with the headlights on, yelling, "What are you kids doing?!" We thought the cops busted us on the first night we drank alcohol. Cochise's father gave us our first reality check.

Drinking was new to us so we got pretty wasted. We didn't realize the effects of alcohol on our bodies and our own limitations. After all the laughter subsided, we decided to head for the tents to sleep it off. I remember waking up in the morning wondering why it was so dark out. Then I noticed that there was something on my face. Apparently during the night our tent fell down. When we crawled out Larry said his back felt like it was on fire. When he pulled up his shirt, we saw that he had cuts all over his back.

"It took me awhile, Henry, but then I realized it was all those tree roots everyone dragged me across."

Around the Fourth of July everyone would get ladyfingers, salutes, cherry bombs, and M-80s and head on down to the Rocks.

The M-80s had a wax covering, so we could throw them in the trench and watch them sink and explode like depth chargers. All the frogs, snakes, even water bugs headed for the other side of the trench out of range from our explosives. The Rocks bordered the Trench and the Trench had a fence around it. We'd take the cap off the line pole, throw a cherry bomb in, then throw a golf ball on top of the cherry bomb. The cherry bomb explodes, sending the golf ball straight up and out of sight. It was fun to watch.

Big Smackum was throwing ladyfingers at everyone until Big Z put a salute under Big Smackum's foot to neutralize the threat. Before Big Z went home, he stuffed a ladyfinger in one of his cigarettes just in case Big Smackum hit him up for one. When Big Z said he was leaving, Big Smackum asked for a cigarette just as Big Z thought. When Smackum lit it up, it started fizzing and sparking. He threw it as it exploded. As I recall, he didn't bum any more cigarettes that night. Being young, everything was a learning experience. Glad we survived life's learning process with our eyes and fingers.

I guess our immature brains thought we were invincible.

Larry's brain was invisible. The Windsor Park Boys took up a collection to see if he'd jump into the trench with his clothes on in the month of March. Larry was always up for a dare.

"Yeah, I was a little short on cash for cigarettes, so I accepted their dare. Man, I can tell you the water temperature is pretty cold in March!"

Just up from the Rocks was the textile mill's pumphouse. There is an eight-inch ledge around one side of the building the Windsor Park Boys would dare each other to cross. Forty feet below the ledge was the Pawtuxet River. Kind of scary to cross when you're just a kid. Rider gave it a go ... and froze right in the middle. Big Z and Cochise had to go out there to get him.

One day at the Rocks, after eating and drinking too much, my intestines told me I had to relieve myself, like, right now. So, off I went into the thick brush to do my business. When I came back, I laughed and told Larry I'd had the best bowel movement of my life. He said, "By the looks of the back of your pants, you're probably right." Apparently my first bowel movement in the woods would be an embarrassing and learning experience. Make sure you get your pants out of the way.

We liked hanging out at the Rocks so much, we'd make excuses just to go there. Big Z had a nightly curfew, but on Ash Wednesday he would go to the Rocks to receive his ashes. A bunch of us would meet at the Rocks to have a fire and stay out later. After hanging out and just before going home, we'd put ashes from our fire on each other's forehead to make it look like we all went to the Ash Wednesday service at church. I guess bonding with the Windsor Park Boys on Ash Wednesday consummated our first day of Lent.

NINTH GRADE

I wasn't happy about going to ninth grade. My mom signed me up for the Seminary. She must have thought I was priest material. Even though I was young, reserved, and didn't know what I wanted to do in life, I knew that I liked girls. Coming from Saint Mary's Grade School where boys and girls were taught by nuns, to a Catholic seminary which only allowed boys, was a tough pill to swallow.

The summer before I went, I told my mom I didn't want to go because I liked girls. She said, "Try the Seminary for a year and see how you like it."

My mom also talked to Larry's mom and convinced her it would be good for the both of us to try it.

Well the Catholic priests who taught school at the Seminary didn't know what they were in for. On the first day of school Larry convinced me to have a thumb war with him in the corridor and the students started to crowd around. When we had a big enough crowd Larry started screaming, "I'm going to kick your ass, fight, fight, fight!" The crowd joined in, "Fight, fight!" About four priests and the vice principal of the Seminary came sprinting down the hallway to break up the fight. The looks on their faces were priceless when they saw what we were doing. It wasn't a happy face. Larry, the risk-taker, got us signed up to build a stone wall on the Seminary grounds. During certain days we were allowed to roam the Seminary grounds for hours. We were told not to talk and just walk around and meditate.

"Yeah, Henry, we were told to mellow out, score some clean air, and just look for some answers, man. Thank God I brought those cigars with me that day."

Larry and I knew some of the girls from St. Mary's School would be at an amusement park at one o'clock. The Seminary bordered Narragansett Bay and we could see the amusement park from the shoreline. We quietly walked along the shoreline from the Seminary to the park. We said hello to the girls, then snuck back to get the bus. To our dismay, Father O'Donnell was waiting for us. He knew we'd left the Seminary grounds and that was breaking the rules. He made us call our parents to let them know we were taking the late bus home because we were volunteering to help build the rock wall—again!

Our lockers were on the second floor. Larry found a hole in the bottom of his locker that went to the ceiling vent in the classroom on the first floor. Every now and then, when Larry was alone, he spoke into the hole pretending to be God. He would call out to the classroom below, saying, "This is the Lord your God." The acoustics were perfect in that locker. There was a deep rumbling sound that echoed into the classroom below. Larry got caught when someone in the classroom asked, "What do you want us to do, Lord?"

In 1967 we learned some valuable lessons at the Catholic seminary that would guide us in life, but we still had the girl virus. I guess once contracted, there was just no vaccine to stop it. So, at the end of the school year we had our parents take us out.

DRIVING CARS

One night, at fifteen years old, my brother and I pushed my father's car down the road, then started it up and drove around the block. To sneak it back, we turned the car off on a small hill about a half block away from our house and coasted it back into the driveway.

At sixteen I remember taking my road test. The Department of Motor Vehicles' driving teacher Mr. McCarthy said, "Are you ready?" I said, "Yup," adjusted my mirrors, and gunned my father's car down the road and around the corner. He started screaming at me, "Oh! Where's the fire?!" When he said "fire," he scared the life out of me. I thought a fire truck was coming, so I hit the brakes and almost put him through the windshield. In the sixties no one wore seatbelts. Mr. McCarthy seemed pretty shaken up. I can only imagine what he's been through giving road tests to all us kids for all those years. He asked me who taught me how to drive. I told him my dad taught me. He said my dad gave me his lead foot and I needed to slow the HELL down. Never thought I'd pass my road test after that, but I took it real slow and he passed me.

We were ready to drive. Windsor Park never saw so many Windsor Park Boys with cars. Throw in an eight-track tape player with some giant rear speakers and Windsor Park could hear us coming a mile away. Being old enough to finally drive was a special moment. It's a proven fact that male drivers are the worst drivers. The Windsor Park Boys backed up those statistics. Little Smackum never even got out of Windsor Park with his parents' '56 Pontiac without getting into a fender bender. Mad Mike had a way with cars too. My dad had a nice 1964 Pontiac Catalina until Mike got ahold of it. He sideswiped it from end to end. Dad was a little upset that day.

After that, Mad Mike got his own car, a 1957 Chevy. One rainy day, while cruising around in his Chevy, a school bus suddenly stopped in front of us without putting on any flashing lights. Mike hit the brakes but we kept going forward. We learned about hydroplaning as we slid into the empty bus. When you hydroplane, you slide on water and don't leave any skid marks. The only skid marks left that day were in my underwear. Well there wasn't any damage to the bus, so Mad Mike and the bus driver decided it was in their best interest to do nothing. The Chevy still ran but the grill and lights were damaged.

The hood was pushed in and wouldn't close. We found some twine and tied it shut. On the way home, Mad Mike was screaming down this large hill, hitting bumps and holes. Consequently, the twine broke, and the hood popped up and smashed the windshield and dented the roof. By the time we got that Chevy home, it looked like someone went around the car with a hammer. I thought the vein on my father's forehead was going to pop.

Elvis asked a friend, Big D, if he could drive his brand-new 1967 Camaro. It was canary yellow with a black vinyl top and had a 350 engine. This car was boss. While Elvis was laying some rubber down over a hill, the car skidded off the road and rolled down an embankment. Big D landed on top of him. Other than cuts and bruises, everybody was okay. The car was totaled, though.

I think being male, and a Windsor Park Boy, only brought our bad driving statistics even higher.

Downtown Artic was West Warwick's local shopping center. It was a great place to show off your car and check out girls too.

"Rider was giving String Bean and I a ride through Artic in his 1964 maroon Pontiac GTO."

String Bean is our Scottish Windsor Park Boy. He lived in the older section of Windsor Park. We called him String Bean because he was ungracefully thin and tall.

It was raining pretty heavy and we were coming up to a GTX, stopped at a red light. By the time Rider saw the GTX it was too late. We skidded right into the back of it. I'm glad nobody got hurt. I remember trying to step on the brakes for him. Too bad I was in the backseat. The GTO split the GTX's trunk like an egg and put a huge dent in the lower frame. The insurance company totaled it.

Rider's GTO was drivable but had so much damage the auto-body guy told him it couldn't be repaired.

Rider's insurance rate skyrocketed. From that point on, Rider gave half his paycheck to the insurance company.

When String Bean and I asked him why he didn't see the car in time, Rider said, "I was watching a raindrop on the windshield."

We started laying down rubber and smoking the tires on the roads all around Windsor Park.

"Yeah, that was boss. We were hot-dogging it all through the town."

Two weeks after I received my driver's license, my father's friend ratted on me when he saw me lighting up my father's Catalina tires. My father told me he knew it was true because everything in his trunk had slid backwards into a pile. I lost my license for two weeks and got reminded that tires cost money.

"Larry, remember when you decided to smoke your tires around the block? You tried power-braking your car to make one connected black tire mark. It would have been a record for sure. You only got thirty feet before my neighbor came out of his house screaming. I could barely see or hear him because of the smoke and screeching tires. It wasn't until you let off the gas that I heard, 'What the hell is wrong with you, are you missing some brain cells?'"

As kids, we were in our own little world and thought we could do whatever we wanted to. Thank God there were grownups around.

Larry was the king of getting stuck. He got stuck in the mud, stuck in a ditch, stuck on a beach. It didn't matter where he went, you were always taking a chance riding with him. One night, Larry decided to explore this dirt road in the country. Of course, we broke down in the middle of nowhere. It was pitch-dark out. The road had no streetlights and cell phones weren't invented yet. We walked about a mile before we finally found a house. We knocked on the door and scared the hell out of this lady. We told her our situation, and asked to use her phone. She handed Larry a phone, which had a long cord attached, outside her door. Before Larry could call his dad, a guy's voice came from a dark room in the house and said, "What are you guys doing out here so late?" That sent chills up our spine. We felt like we were in a horror movie.

Larry hurried up and told his father where we were. His dad said he'd send someone out to pick us up. Whoever he sent never found us, and five of us slept out in Larry's mosquito-infested car that night. Larry's father's garage guy found us the next morning. Apparently, it was a loose battery cable. He tightened it and the car started right up. Till this day, this is the first thing I check when my car doesn't start.

Larry thought it would be fun driving on the Division Road sand dunes. We let some air out of the tires and drove his 1963 Chevy Impala up the first large hill we could find. King Larry of Stuck did it again. The car bottomed out right at the top. Cochise and some Windsor Park Boys were driving on Route 95 and spotted Larry's vehicle stuck on top of the sand dune. They said from a distance it looked like a toy car on top of a mound of sand. They came to our rescue. Cochise and the Windsor Park Boys couldn't believe how high up the sand dune we were. They started to laugh when they noticed Larry's car rocked like a seesaw. His right front tire and left back tire didn't touch the ground. The Windsor Park Boys rocked the Chevy back and forth. Larry and I felt like we were sitting on the launch pad of the *Space Shuttle* waiting to take off. Our feet were up by our face. I could feel the car starting to dislodge. All of a sudden, we went screaming down the dune in reverse. I thought the car was going to flip over. I could feel pressure across my body.

"When we got to the bottom, Henry had to check his shorts."

"Did not, Larry!"

"Henry, I remember doing donuts with my cars." Find a dirt or snowy parking lot and spin that car in a circle! Elvis and Big D said they could film me doing donuts and fishtailing in the mill parking lot. The lot was covered with snow. This would be on film forever. Who could pass this up? The parking lot was empty and huge. So, I went speeding into the parking lot with Cochise riding shotgun. I started waving and laughing as we went by the guys filming. Then, I tried to put the car into a spin only to realize it wasn't going to spin. I turned the steering wheel both ways. We kept going straight, picking up speed. Now we're heading for a giant snowbank, but I wasn't worried because it was only snow. It felt like forever to smash into that snowbank. Well, little did we know, not only was the parking lot full of snow-covered ice, but the snowbank was iced over too. The only impression I made that day was on my Impala's hood and grill. This was the first time I realized that ice is an all-around bad thing. I also found out later there was no film in the movie camera.

"Larry, I'll never forget my 1964 Ford Mustang. That car was cherry, until Cochise's milkshake fiasco." I was parked across the street from Cochise's house watching him throw water balloons at the windshields of the Windsor Park Boys as they drove by. Only this time Cochise decided to throw his milkshake. When it hit the windshield, the driver lost control, fishtailed on Cochise's lawn, and shot across the road right into my recently bought '64 Mustang.

Another irresponsible thing we did was jousting. No horses, no lances, no suit of armor, and no prize money. Just cars, water balloons, squirt guns, and bragging rights. We'd drive around the plat trying to catch our opponent off guard, especially as they tried to re-load their squirt guns and water balloons. One tournament Cochise was driving with Mad Mike as shotgun and Larry was driving me. We bombarded Cochise and Mad Mike for hours. Larry and I thought the jousting was over, so we pulled alongside Cochise's iron horse to start the bragging rights. When Larry rolled down his window, they threw a dozen eggs all over us and the car. As hysterical as it looked, Larry, embarrassed with egg dripping from his face, walked over to Cochise's car, grabbed his antenna, and turned it into a pretzel. After the egg cooked on Larry's face, we all had a good laugh.

Lucky thing we were jousting with older vehicles. Unbeknownst to us, the chemical composition of egg yolk eats through the clear coat on the surface of car paint, only to stain the paint if it isn't removed quickly. Another of life's lessons we learned the hard way as we grew up.

One day in 1968, Larry was in one of his exploring moods and drove a bunch of us onto Route 95 when it was being rebuilt into Interstate 95. It was a Sunday, so the construction companies weren't working on it. Construction vehicles and equipment were parked all along the highway. Route 95 was still gravel and no one was around. Every cement bridge abutment had wooden ramps for the construction trucks to get over them. We even had to find wood to put on some abutments to get over them. We must have gotten five miles down the unfinished highway before a cop noticed and stopped us.

He came up to our window and said to Larry, "Where do you think you're going, this highway is closed!" Of course, Larry, with a straight face, said, "Oh, I didn't know it was closed, Officer." The expression on that cop's face was priceless. We couldn't keep from laughing. He told us not to be wise guys and gave us an escort off the highway until we hit a paved road.

I'll never forget the day I was riding around and saw one of the Windsor Park Boys' vehicles in front of me, stopped at a red light. All of a sudden, the trunk cracked open a little, and a hand started waving at me.

"Guess who it was, Larry."

"Ah! Me?"

Another time, Larry, the King of Fun, suggested that we do a trunk stuff. Sushi, one of the younger Windsor Park Boys who we nicknamed by shortening his last name, String Bean, and I jammed ourselves into Larry's car trunk. Sushi was on the bottom. As soon as we heard the trunk latch click, Sushi started freaking out. Larry jumped into the car and started driving around Windsor Park. The trunk light was flickering like a strobe light and all you could see was the look of terror in Sushi's eyes. Since that day, if anyone mentioned a trunk stuff or teased to throw Sushi in the trunk, it brought the same look of fear to Sushi's face and he'd start running.

The Windsor Park Boys snuck into many a drive-in movie by hiding in the trunk of a car. Except Sushi—he was a paying customer.

Mooning: to expose one's buttocks to someone in order to amuse them.

In the sixties mooning was popular at American universities. Riding around mooning everyone was a popular fad with the Windsor Park Boys too. We'd do anything for a laugh. Big Smackum wasn't shy with his butt. The first time everyone saw his butt was on the way to Scarborough Beach. Four cars of Windsor Park Boys and Girls were on the way to the beach, when the last car in the caravan started passing us all. Their horn was blaring and someone's ass was hanging out the window. Everyone in their car was yelling "mooner." One of the girls said she wasn't sure who that was. I told her maybe it's because all you could see was a hairy ass smiling at you. Big Smackum's ass was seen all around town. "Everyone tried mooning, wouldn't you say, Larry?"

HIGH SCHOOL

ost of the Windsor Park Boys went to West Warwick High School. High school was hard enough for most of us—especially getting used to all the different personalities, and kids bullying you. Larry made high school fun. He got into a lot of trouble but he made us laugh. He was the class clown who didn't worry about anything. Larry could lighten up any situation. He had some kid call our classroom phone in the middle of history class. Larry was next to the phone sharpening a pencil. When the phone started ringing, Larry told the teacher, "Hold on I have to take this." He answers the phone and says, "What! Really!" He then hangs up the phone and says, "Duty calls." He rips his shirt and pants off to reveal a Superman costume with cape and boots included.

The class went into hysterics, laughing and screaming, "It's Superman!" Larry took off running around the classroom and into the hallway with his hands extended like he was flying. We saw him run by the classroom twice. Once with two teachers on his heels, then with the Vice Principal joining in. Each time he went by the classroom everyone would scream, "Look up in the sky! It's a bird! It's a plane!" Larry yelled back, "It's Superman!"

During lunch, nobody would sit at our table in the cafeteria. Why? Because nobody wanted to get blamed for all the forks sticking in the drop ceiling above it.

Vice Principal Crabtree had the dubious chore of walking around during lunchtime making sure there was law and order. The ceiling was so high he never thought to look up. We'd be talking to the Vice Principal for a while, but as he turned around to scan the cafeteria, Larry would put the top of the fork on his fingertips face up, and the handle at his wrist. When he started throwing the fork upward, he would grab his forearm to catapult the fork into the ceiling tiles.

When everyone at the table started laughing, Crabtree would spin around really quick to see if we were doing something wrong. For the longest time he couldn't figure out what we were laughing about. A week and twelve forks in the ceiling later, he accidently found out. One of the forks decided to dislodge from the ceiling tiles and almost hit him in the head. We all started to snicker. He looked up, saw the forks, then stared right at us. You could see everything in his head starting to click. Everyone at the table lost their smiles really quick. I'd say we were looking pretty guilty. We gave him the "we really didn't mean any harm" eyes, but it didn't work. He took a pad and pencil out of his pocket, then calmly told us he was writing our names in for detention for two weeks starting tomorrow.

Larry loved to pick on Vice Principal Crabtree, especially during lunchtime.

"I guess I would do anything for a laugh, Henry."

"Sometimes you went a little too far, Larry."

Larry started talking to Crabtree during lunch, apologizing for the fork incident. Then when Crabtree turned away, he stuck his fingers in his vanilla ice cream and flicked it all over the back of the Vice Principal's suit jacket. All the knuckleheads in the school would laugh. Larry fed off all the laughter and kept doing it. When the laughter started, Crabtree looked up only to find nothing stuck in the ceiling.

This went on until Martha Kelly (the F-Bomb Queen) noticed Crabtree's jacket. She waited and caught Larry Collins flicking his ice cream, getting his laughs at the Vice Principal's expense. She walked right up to Crabtree and squealed on him.

"Henry, remember when I got even with Martha?"

"Yeah, Larry, at my expense!"

We were at our lockers when Larry told me to do as he said. He told me to extend my hand out about chest high. So, I did. Then to extend it out further and a little lower. So, I did. Then, he said to spin completely around real fast. I didn't realize the F-bomb Queen was standing right behind me trying to listen in on our conversation. When I spun around, my hand hit her right in the breast. I was mortified, she was mortified, then Martha's F-bombs started to explode. Of course, Larry laughed his butt off. A week later, Larry met an Italian exchange student at school who could barely speak English. He noticed him checking out Martha. Larry told him, if you like her you should go up to her and say, "I want to bang you." He said it was a compliment and it's what a woman likes to hear. We all watched as he marched up to Martha. I didn't know whose facial expression to watch, Martha's or Larry's. Martha slapped him so hard it could have sent him back to Italy. He walked back over to us and said, "She no like me." Martha saw Larry laughing. She knew there was a good chance Larry had put him up to it.

"Larry, remember when our school had that unexpected assembly in the auditorium?"

"Yeah, Henry, when the Vice Principal walked up on the stage you could see the vein on his forehead ready to pop."

Our school basketball team had just played a game at another school. The game was broadcast live on our local radio station. He said he was very upset at what he heard on the radio. Crabtree said, "Every time the crowd thought a referee made a bad call against our school, you'd hear a chant from the crowd. The chant went like this: "Munch, munch, munch, the ref brought his lunch-eat it, ref, eat it!"

Of course, when he said that to the assembly over the school PA system, everyone in the auditorium laughed their heads off. He then said, "It's always that one percent of the students that gives our school a bad name." I think we owe Mr. Crabtree an apology.

LET THE GOOD TIMES ROLL

In the seventies most of us turned eighteen. Our hair started getting longer. We wanted to grow beards and mustaches. We wanted to be different.

Some of us didn't have too much facial hair, so a bunch of us decided to put eyebrow pencil on our peach fuzz and head to the mall. We were all having fun looking like Zorro until the bullies of the school showed up. We got our beans busted. After that embarrassing incident we waited until nature took its course.

Everyone dressed in bellbottom pants, tie-dye shirts, head-bands, and beads. The girls had miniskirts, maxi dresses, and peasant blouses. We were listening to Creedence, The Beatles, The Rolling Stones, Led Zeppelin, ZZ Top, Foreigner, Alice Cooper, Steppenwolf, Pink Floyd, Black Sabbath, Deep Purple, Aerosmith, The Who, the Eagles, AC/DC, Queen, Jethro Tull, and tons of other rock bands.

It just so happened that in the spring of 1971, Rhode Island made all of us minors into legal adults by lowering the drinking age to eighteen. The good times were about to roll. After working, we'd get together, listen to some music, have a few brews and some-times a couple of tokes of weed.

"Henry, remember the night you partied in Windsor Park and you fell asleep in your car?"

"I remember my car door slamming, then seeing Frenchie, the Z's sister's boyfriend, asleep in my car. I remember saying to myself, 'I'll let him stay in my car to sleep it off,' then I ran into the house."

I was sitting on the sofa when a woman came up to me and said, "Henry?" I said, "Yeah." By this time, I had one eye open and said to myself, "My mom doesn't wear glasses." That's when I heard someone scream, "Henry Perkins!" I accidently ran into Bambino's parents' house, which is across the street from Cochise's house and up the street from my parents' house. Bambino was the youngest Windsor Park Boy. They have a son named Henry too. My other eye gazed down the hallway watching her husband in his underwear, bouncing off the walls trying to put his pants on.

When he came up to me I closed my eyes waiting for the impact (once again). Thank God he recognized me before he started smashing my head in. He asked me what I was doing in his house. Of course, my response was, "I don't know." Most of the houses in Windsor Park were ranch houses that looked alike.

"No excuse, Henry."

"It all seemed like a dream to me, Larry." He asked me, "Have you been drinking?" I repeated, "Yeah." I told them I was sorry and off I went. You could hear them laughing as I left the house.

Bambino came over to my house the next morning and said his parents would have the outside light on and the coffee brewing, just in case I decided to stop over tonight. "That was really understanding of them, Larry."

Happy Valley was our hidden-away party spot. It was further in the woods. One had to cross rotted wood beams near the mill's pumphouse, then travel down a narrow path that had water on one side and a steep drop-off on the other side. It took a while just to get to Happy Valley. We used to bust up Bambino because on the way down to the party, he would fall off the path, and after the party, on the way back, he would walk straighter than all of us. We could make all the noise we wanted. Nobody wanted to walk that far to investigate the noise, especially at night. Great place to throw a loud party.

"Larry, remember my nineteenth birthday party in my parents' backyard?" The drinking age was lowered to eighteen that year. We started having a drinking contest. Not sure where Frenchie was putting all that beer. We started to think he had a hollow leg. He drank over a case of beer. Older Smackum brother drank a lot too. We were all watching him put away all those beers, wondering what was keeping him upright. All of a sudden in midsentence while talking with my mom, he fell right out of his chair.

We had a band playing. There were lots of clams and corn on the cob to eat. During the night around 2 am, we did sneak out to a late-night diner for some more food and coffee. We filed into the diner one by one, sitting at the table. The waitress came over and was about to take our order, when she noticed Rider just entering the diner. He was stone-faced drunk. He tried hurrying up to get to our table, stumbled past everyone, fell backwards across the aisle into some chairs and onto the floor under a table. The waitress looked at him, then looked at us and said, "Is he with you?"

Larry said, "I never saw him in my life." Everyone burst into hysterics.

Rider entertained everyone that night by stumbling into the Windsor Park Hall of Shame. It's an exclusive club. You really have to mess up and make us laugh to get in.

One night, while drinking at the Falcon Club, we dared the bartender, who was a little older than us, to tend the bar with no clothes on. He laughed but refused. The Windsor Park Boys were ball-busters and always daring each other to do things. We bought the bartender a bunch of shots and beers and kept daring him. As the night progressed he wouldn't budge. Now and then he'd say "piss call for the bartender" and disappear into the men's room. It wasn't until the fifth piss call that the shots and beers changed his mind. He walked out of the men's room naked as a newborn. The guys were laughing, the girls were giggling. He tended the bar like it was a regular Friday night.

The old guy that lived next door to the club stopped in to have his usual one beer like he did every Friday night. As he walked in, we said hello and acted normal. We all watched him as he walked up to the bar and asked for a beer. His head did a double-take as his mouth dropped to the floor.

The naked bartender guy gave him his nightly beer. It didn't take a genius to figure out everyone in the bar drank a little too much that night. The old guy couldn't finish his beer fast enough.

Before he left he said, "There is something wrong with your generation." Then he shook his head and walked home.

"Larry, remember we dared you to take a carton of cigarettes from a gas station?" Then we all drove by the police station with lit cigarettes sticking out of our mouths and ears, laughing the whole time. You couldn't dare Larry to do something. He was a sick puppy in those days.

"Remember, Larry, when my parents left the house for a long period of time, I'd invite the Windsor Park Boys over to have a few brews?" Drinking was still new to us, and Rider and I had a little too much. We were acting up, so Elvis locked us up in my father's shed to sober up until my older brother, Mad Mike, came home. When he finally arrived, everyone told him what we did and where we were. My brother said, "Oh no! My father has a refrigerator with a full keg of draft beer in there. It has a tap system coming out of the side of the refrigerator!" When they opened the door to the shed, Rider and I nearly fell down just from laughing, never mind from all the beer we drank.

Can't forget the bachelor party near the golf course. Someone called the police because of all the noise. The Windsor Park Boys weren't harming anyone and the nearest house was quite a distance away. The police said to leave the area or they'd be back. The police were about to leave, when one of the officers found an empty beer can in the backseat of their cruiser. They were upset at all the ball busting and laughter and took three of us back to the station. Larry, String Bean, and Bambino were in an office being questioned by the officer. After all the laughing and giggling stopped, the officer started to take String Bean's information for his report.

Going down the incident report he came to eye color. The officer said to String Bean, "Color of your eyes?" String Bean, feeling no pain and never being in a police station before, thought he said "cover up your eyes." He looked at the officer and said, "Well okay." Then he covered up his eyes with his hands. The officer yelled, "What are you, a wise guy?" Everyone laughed so hard the officer locked them all up behind bars for two hours before letting them go. That night, the Windsor Park Boys' Hall of Shame Committee welcomed String Bean as its newest member.

How about the night Sushi was inducted into the Windsor Park Hall of Shame? Boy did he like to party. One night, we decided to just ride around. We saw Sushi coming out of the Windsor Park Club looking like he drank and smoked way too much. We picked him up and decided to ride around in the country on the back roads. You could always tell when Sushi partied too much. His eyes were barely opened.

Sushi said, "I have to take a squirt." So, I pulled over on a dark country road with only farms and fields around us. No streetlights around these roads. It looked like a good place to relieve oneself. When he exited my car, he left the door open, so the dome light on the inside of my car stayed on. We waited, but no Sushi. I yelled for him, but no answer. I got out and walked around the car to see what was keeping him. When I closed the car door, I could see sparks in the distance, then a glimpse of Sushi. Then more sparks and another glimpse of Sushi. It was then I realized I'd stopped my car too close to a hill. Sushi rolled down the incline and landed on an electric cow fence. He was all twisted on the wire. It took me a minute to get him untangled, getting a couple of shocks in the process. Sushi's once squinty eyes, were now as wide as half dollars. If cows could talk, Sushi would be the talk of the farm.

After having a few brews at the Rocks, Big Z and I walked a couple of miles to the Burger Chef. On the way back, we bumped into Big Z's cousin. He showed us his new homemade wooden boat with outboard motor. We were tired of walking so we asked him if he could take us up the Pawtuxet River. It would be a nice scenic short-cut back to the Rocks plus save us time and energy. He couldn't wait to show us how the boat and motor ran. So, we motored up the river. When we got to the drop-off spot, the mill's pumphouse, Big Z and I tried to get out of the boat at the same time. The boat leaned so much, water started gushing over its side, filling up really quick. The homemade boat started sinking motor first. His helpless-looking cousin was still sitting in the seat, trying to bail water out with his hands. That picture of him going down with the boat is still etched in my mind. The outboard motor made a bubbling sound when it finally went under.

To make matters worse, Z's cousin had a brand-new pellet rifle in the boat and lost it when the boat flipped over. It's been in the Pawtuxet River for fifty years now. He's probably still mad at us.

In the seventies, hippie pot was readily available. It mostly came from Mexico and Columbia. At rare times you could buy Panama Red, Maui Wowie, and Jamaican weed. If you smoked pot, you had little tiny round holes burned in your clothes or up-holstery from burning seeds popping.

Pot in the seventies had THC levels of one percent. The pot to-day has THC levels averaging more than six to eight percent. Back then you had to smoke an awful lot of pot to get a buzz. Once you had that buzz, you'd laugh hysterically at the stupidest things; but two and a half hours later, when the buzz wore off, there was no hangover.

One day in his car, Larry, our resident pothead and comedian, lit up some Columbian weed joints and passed them around. He said, "Keep the windows shut," figuring it would help out with the buzz. For some reason pot made you real hungry, so off to the A&W Root Beer to get some food.

Larry was talking like Cheech and Chong during the ride there. He had us laughing our heads off. When we parked at the A&W, we started pooling our money together for food. The car-hop startled the hell out of us when she knocked on the window. Larry rolled the window down to order. We ordered four sodas and four french fries. She laughed and said, "I thought you guys would be hungrier than that!" It wasn't until then that I remem-bered all the smoke in the car. It must have shot-gunned out, hitting her right in the face. I think there was enough smoke in that car to give her a good buzz.

I can only imagine if we had gotten stopped by the police and rolled the window down. In those days pot was illegal, although they didn't seem to arrest individuals with small amounts of pot. We were at a concert in downtown Providence and the arena was reeking with marijuana. People were passing joints up and down the aisles. They would have had to arrest everyone in the place. Now it's legal in a lot of states.

"Henry, remember when I went to see Doctor Yank because I had problems breathing out of my nose?"

He looked up my nostrils with a small flashlight. He said, "I can see some kind of blockage up there." With his flashlight and some tweezers, he started yanking out zigzag paper. Like I don't know who was more freaked out, Dr. Yank or myself. He looked at me and advised me not to snort any more finger-burning roaches.

We have to talk about Frenchie. He was nicknamed after his French-Canadian roots. Frenchie was a Windsor Park Boy ten times over. He's one of those friends you'd look at and just laugh. One funny-looking and -acting guy. He always had his prescription sunglasses on, day or night. Everyone liked being around him. He didn't live in Windsor Park but he dated Big and Little Z's sister. The Z's sister hated when Frenchie hung out with us. We were kind of rough on their relationship. He would always get in trouble being with us. We had him in the doghouse so many times. One time on date night, Frenchie had to stop at the Windsor Park Club to get something and told her he'd be right out. I don't think Z's sister realized the Windsor Park Boys were all hanging out in the club that night.

When Frenchie came in, he told us he couldn't stay because his girl was outside in the car and he was taking her out on a date. Everyone wanted Frenchie to stay and we convinced him to sit and have one quick beer. We all knew Frenchie was very sociable, and when he wasn't looking we'd buy him a couple of cold beers. Eventually the boys bought Frenchie so many beers, the bartender put empty glasses upside down on the bar for every beer bought so they wouldn't get warm. When Frenchie never came out of the club, Z's sister stormed into the club to investigate. Once she saw the Windsor Park Boys she realized the problem. There was Frenchie, at the end of the bar laughing and socializing with all those beers in front of him.

The expression on her face was priceless. The expression on Frenchie's face was like, how did I ever get into this mess?

Frenchie's eyes widened as his girlfriend's folded, sending daggers at him. She said, "Either you leave with me, or it's over!" He just sat there looking at his girlfriend, looking at the Windsor Park Boys, and glancing down at the beers on the bar. There was dead silence, then all you could hear was the sound of her promise ring that Frenchie bought her bouncing off his beer bottles, then spinning around on the floor like a top. Everyone watched as it came to rest. Before she could get out the door, you could hear a low chant, "Frenchie, Frenchie." By the time she got out the door, the chant got louder: "Frenchie! Frenchie!"

He stayed with the Windsor Park Boys that night but had some real making up to do over the next few weeks.

Frenchie got his revenge one night. We had just finished eating and drinking at the club. Frenchie said, "Let me give you a ride in my new vehicle." When we pulled into a store parking lot, Frenchie farted. He was known to kill ants with his farts, but this one could have gagged a maggot. He had everyone choking. "Larry, it hit me like a ton of bricks. I couldn't breathe and started gasping for air. Because it was my first time in Frenchie's new car, I couldn't find the levers for his door or window in time. I projectile-vomited all over his car."

"Henry, payback's a bitch."

Later that summer, Frenchie invited me to one of his family's cookouts. They all started talking about Frenchie's raunchy farts and my projectile vomiting. Frenchie had told them the story, but they wanted the person who suffered to tell it again. I had everyone at the cookout laughing as I told the story, and I assured them that I'd never be caught with Frenchie in an enclosed area. Everyone had a lot to eat at the cookout, and we all stayed upwind of him that night.

In 1973 Frenchie and the Z's sister got married. She probably thought marriage would calm him down and keep him out of trouble.

The story that got Frenchie into the Windsor Park Hall of Shame was the night his wife let him go out with us to a bar just down the street from where they were living. We all had a bunch of laughs and too much to drink. It was during the streaking fad period. Late at night when we left the bar, Frenchie and Larry decided to streak. They went down Main Street with their pants around their ankles and hoo-has flopping in the wind. Like two-year-olds running away from their mother. All of a sudden, Frenchie fell down and Larry landed on top of him. Frenchie's black eyeglass frames broke in half, giving him a large cut between his eyes. The Windsor Park Boys jumped into action and drove him to the hospital. Larry grabbed a wheelchair and ran down the hallway with him while the rest of us made siren noises. We wheeled him to the emergency check-in. The woman behind the desk looked at us, shook her head, and said, "I hate to ask what happened. Just fill this out."

The night ended with us dropping Frenchie off on his doorstep at three o'clock in the morning. He had stitches between his eyes, white hospital tape holding his glasses together, still feeling no pain from all the drinking, and was fumbling with his keys trying to get into the house. Even though we'd had a lot to drink, we realized that there was a slight chance that we shared some of the responsibility for the situation Frenchie was in. So, we blew the car horn until his wife put the outside light on and met him at the front door. Then we sped away.

SPORTS

Some of the best Windsor Park memories happened when we played sports. We played softball for the Falcon Club, a local club in Windsor Park.

During the three years that we played, we only won a single game.

I can still visualize Frenchie pitching one of our Sunday morning games. There he was, standing on the mound, still hung over, wearing his sunglasses. He was pitching a great game until the third inning, when all of a sudden, the batter hit a line drive right back at him. It hit him right in the hoo-ha! The field was packed with spectators. Everyone let out a gasp.

Ever hear the phrase "nut up or shut up"? Frenchie just stood there like a wounded warrior. You could see the pain in his face. He never said a word and never grabbed his hoo-ha. He just turned around, walked off gingerly into centerfield, and fell down over an embankment, out of sight. It took another inning before Mr. Balls of Steel reappeared. Everyone was glad to hear the jewels were still in the family. Frenchie and his purple one-eyed Willie were the talk of the field that morning.

Paul Johnson

Another sport for us to bond was playing tackle football. One day the bullies of the high school saw us playing in the park and challenged us to a game. They were stronger, muscle-head-type guys. What they lacked in brain power, they made up in brute strength. They bullied us in high school and saw an opportunity to do it again, physically and legally on the field. Of course, we accepted their challenge.

The game was mismatched. We couldn't stop their running game. They knew they were too strong for us. They had arms like our legs and legs like our bodies. Larry was fast enough to get in on the tackles but lacked the weight to get them down on the ground. They were dragging him down the field.

A friend of the Windsor Park Boys we called Big D was the biggest guy on our team. He was huge but a slow runner. We figured when Larry grabbed ahold of the bully around the legs, to slow him down, Big D had enough time to get there and knock him over like a bowling pin. When the game was almost over and they knew we were going to lose, they started their verbal bullying and taunting like they usually did. We needed to make a final statement. The bullying must stop, right now, on this field. From now on if you run with the ball, you pay the price. After the first bully got smashed, you could see a little fear in their eyes. The greatest moment of the game was when Peter the Great, the most arrogant, biggest bully of the school, ran with the football. He had a couple bullies blocking for him, but we had Larry the Weasel, who snuck around his blockers and grabbed Peter around his legs. Peter must have dragged Larry twenty yards before Larry slowed him down. Then, Peter had nowhere to go. He stood there waiting and watching as Big D steamrolled in for some Windsor Park Boy payback.

Big D hit him high and Frenchie finished him off on the way down. They put him into La La Land. One bully over easy the hard way. They knocked him out cold. It took him a minute before he came around. The misunderstood bullies finally understood that the Windsor Park Boys weren't doormats. No wiping your feet here! We could take it and we could give it right back. Even though we lost the game, they knew the Windsor Park Boys were a bunch of guys that gave it all they had. At the end of the game the bullies reluctantly shook our hands and said, "Nice game." They actually showed us a little respect. Respect that went a long way. It looked like a turning point for Peter and the bullies.

THE GREAT SIGN WAR

(not recommended)

Having no responsibility and all the time in the world brought on The Great Sign War. Take a sign, put it in front of your friend's house, and play dumb. Rule: never take an important sign that might endanger someone. One night, Larry and I tried to get a speed-limit sign, but it didn't turn out so well. As Larry shimmied up the four-by-four wooden pole with a crowbar that we got from my trunk, a couple of police officers pulled up behind the car. The trunk was wide open and we had a blinking yellow sawhorse-looking caution sign in there that we took from a construction site. Before they got out of their cruiser, Larry quickly threw the crowbar away as I slammed the trunk shut. I recognized one of the officers. He was an older Windsor Park Boy graduate named Tardy.

I thought knowing Tardy would work to our advantage. We needed to get out of this mess. Our conversation started off, "Hey Tardy, how you been?" Then, it went into Tardy saying, "What are you guys doing? Trying to take a sign?" Of course, we said, "Who us, Tardy? Not us." Then he asked, "What's in the trunk?" He must have caught a glimpse of the sign but he couldn't get in there. We said, "Nothing." All of a sudden, the trunk latch clicked and the trunk slowly lifted open by itself. Larry and I stood there in disbelief. The blinking light glowing from the trunk captured the two officers laughing their heads off.

Tardy asked what we were going to do with it. We explained it was going to Windsor Park to be put in front of the Smackum brothers' house as a joke. The Windsor Park Boy graduate looked at us, smiled, and said, "I can't let you take this, you know." We said, "We know, sorry about all this." Tardy took the sign and they let us go.

"Larry, remember that plywood liquor sign you wanted really bad?"

The sign was about twelve feet long, four feet in height, and was fastened to a chain-link fence with heavy wire every four inches. Larry pleaded with us to help him unfasten it, but it looked like way too much work.

"Like, man, I worked on that sign at night during the weekends and still couldn't get it unfastened."

The next weekend Frenchie and I were out riding around scouting the sign situation. We saw a State Police sign on a four-by-four-inch wooden pole. It was about a hundred yards from the barracks. I was laughing while mentioning to Frenchie that it would look good in front of Larry's house. Before I could say any more, Frenchie drove his old car into the wooden pole, breaking it in half. Clearly, we weren't thinking too good, because we drove by the barracks with the sign in the trunk and four feet of wooden pole sticking out.

"Larry, we laughed all the way to your parents' house. We stuck the sign in the bushes under your window."

"Yeah like, the next morning my mom got a call from our next-door neighbor asking if we'd turned our home into a State Police Barracks."

Mom said, "What are you talking about?"

The neighbor said, "Go out and stand in your front yard." After the shock kicked in, my mom looked at me like I had something to do with it.

Remember phone booths—a glass box with a public pay phone? It had a light that lit the booth up at night. The Windsor Park Boys had the base of the booth all unbolted. All that was needed was for someone to cut the wires coming from the telephone pole. Nobody wanted to cut the wires. Not sure where the booth was going to go, but everyone decided to leave it alone. One of the Windsor Park Boys' better choices growing up.

GIRLS

String Bean's first time being curious with a girl happened at the Rocks. He was all over one of the Windsor Park Girls when all of a sudden, he heard someone behind him say, "What on earth do you think you're doing?" One of the mothers from Windsor Park was looking for her daughter and caught String Bean, red-faced and red-handed. She told the girl to go home and laid into String Bean. String Bean was so scared that someone would tell the girl's older brother of his actions, he stayed in the woods until dark because he feared getting beaten up. When he finally got home, his mother asked him why he was so late. He told his mother he lost track of the time.

Having fun with the guys created a lot of memories, but girls started to get our attention. If girls came with a handbook, I didn't know about it. I would have read it dozens of times. When it came to girls, I was dumb as a stump. I hung around the guys way too much. By the time I was interested in girls, most of them in and around Windsor Park were either married or spoken for. This is what happens when you're a late-bloomer.

One day, Little Smackum asked a girl out on a date, but she wouldn't go with him unless he got a date for her girlfriend. Of course, Little Smackum thought of the late-bloomer. Little Smackum was noted for going with rather large girls. He begged me to double-date with him. I told him I never went on a blind date and didn't trust him. (I didn't want any big surprises.)

He said, "Don't worry, just come with me on this date!" Of course, it turned out just as I'd suspected. His date was large and mine was extra-large.

He drove us to a drive-in movie. My first thought was, well this isn't bad. I'm in the backseat of a car at a drive-in late at night. Even though my date wasn't exactly my type, she was a real nice person. Well, after having a few beers my nice date started getting really friendly. Before I knew what was happening, she was all over me and started dry-humping me. She had Smackum's car bouncing up and down like a lowrider. I heard Little Smackum say, "What the hell." He looked back wondering why his head kept hitting the car roof. Just when I thought I was ready to black out, I yelled out, "Snack bar!" Suddenly the car came to a rest. She said, "You want to go to the snack bar?" With one lung I said, "Oh yeah." As we exited the car, about ten cars started flashing their lights on and off. They started screaming, "Whoa, baby! Rock that car!"

The following weekend, he tried to make it up to me by taking me to a club in downtown Providence. I made sure I had a bunch of beer in me before we left Windsor Park, in case there were any more surprises. By the time we got to Providence, I was feeling no pain. This was the first time we went to a club in Rhode Island's capital. Smackum saw a woman walking into a club and said, "Let's try this place." So, we pulled over and went in. The club was very dark inside. It took a while before your eyes got adjusted to it. While at the bar enjoying another drink, Little Smackum started kicking me in the shins, almost breaking my leg. He motioned me to look across the bar. Two younger guys were making out. I looked at Smackum like, "You did it again." He picked the wrong club. We were looking for girls. We started downing our drinks faster. Suddenly, a girl sat down next to me. I could hear music playing in the other room. So, I asked her to dance and she agreed. We walked into the dark room and started slow-dancing. Then I noticed we were the only mixed couple. It was time to leave. Before we ran out, the girl told us she waitressed at a small restaurant in Providence and we should stop in tomorrow. Little Smackum insisted we should visit this girl. So, we stopped by the restaurant the next day. Apparently, not only was the club really dark last night but we must have drank way too much. This girl was a lot older than us and she looked like she fell out of the ugly tree and hit every branch on the way down. Her front teeth stuck straight out of her head. She could have eaten corn on the cob through a picket fence. The rest of her teeth were missing.

By the way the restaurant owner and his wife were treating us, she must have told them we were the gay couple she met at the club last night. Little Smackum strikes again.

In life one has to find out who you are and who you are not. What you want and what you don't want. I want to thank Little Smackum for that.

One night, Little Smackum met us at this crowded lounge over a bowling alley. He surprised everyone and brought a drop-dead petite blonde. We were all jealous of him. It looked like he had a breakthrough moment with girls. This girl was a knockout. Little Smackum was all smiles as he pulled the chair out for the little blonde princess. Then for some reason he kept pulling the chair back and never got the chair back to her in time. The princess was dethroned. She was stripped of her title as her bottom came crashing to the floor. She was beyond mortified. It all went downhill after that. The breakthrough moment was over. The princess abdicated and Little Smackum never saw her again.

I really didn't know how to speak to girls. I met a girl who said her name was Billy Joe. I told her she looked like a Billy Joe. That remark got her away from me in two seconds. I scared a beautiful dark-skinned girl away from me when I told her I watched *Soul Train* on TV. I just didn't know how to act or put roses around my words.

"Henry, remember when you finally got a date and we doubled in your car, when all of a sudden you farted and said the gun went off officially starting the beer-guzzling contest."

"Yeah, Larry, that was the same night our dates officially

stopped seeing us."

Big Z and I double-dated with a couple of beautiful girls from high school. After the date we decided to take the girls to Lovers' Lane to park and make out. This night I decided to go from first base to second base. While Big Z and his date were making out in the backseat, I decided to make my move. The first slap to my face was cushioned by the drink I had earlier in the night. Big Z and his date didn't pay attention and were still making out. The second slap to my face got my attention, as there was no cushion to absorb that blow. Big Z and his date laughed their heads off, saying, "What the hell you doing up there?" We all laughed and the thrill was over. I excused myself to go pee and when I came back, the romantic cave-man that I was, told her I wrote her name in the snow, and it looked like her handwriting. She assured me it wasn't her handwriting. My ball-busting and dating skills didn't get me another date with her.

Little Z was also a late-bloomer. He was fixed up on a blind date with a girl named Suzie, who just came out of a bad relationship. Little Z wanted my date and me to double-date for moral support. When he picked her up at her front door, she was reluctant to leave the house. Her mother pushed her out the door and said, "Go out and have some fun." I could tell by the look on Suzie's face, the planets were not aligned that night. Little Z took us to the local amusement park. He bought her some popcorn, cotton candy, and soda. She told Little Z that she wanted to go home because she was feeling sick. He convinced her to stay and enjoy the rest of the night. The first ride we went on was

"Tilt-a-Whirl." His date didn't stand a chance. This ride spun clockwise, counterclockwise, tilted up on end, and spun around like a top. When the ride was over, his date turned into Suzie Satan like in the movie *The Exorcist*. Her projectile-vomiting mouth started saying swears I couldn't repeat. The amusement park wasn't so amusing anymore. So Little Z decided to take Suzie Satan home. When we pulled up to her mom's house, he kept the car running, put it in neutral, and just put the emergency brake on to keep it from rolling. Little Z tried to walk around the car to open up her door. Suzie Satan was already halfway out the door when the parking brake decided to let go and we started rolling away slowly down the road. I was in the backseat with my date. So, there we were, watching his date holding on to the door and front seat, slowly dragging her down the road screaming her vulgar head off, saying, "What is this, the grand F-bomb finale?"

Little Z ran back around the car and stopped the runaway vehicle. As she limped up the walkway to her front door in her ruined shoes, bleeding from her knee with puke all over her ripped clothing, she started screaming at Little Z, "Stay right where you are! I'll get the front door by myself!" Her mom opened the door and asked, "Did you have a good time?" All we could hear was the F-bomb going off. As we drove off, my date and I couldn't help but laugh all the way home. The double date we'll all never forget.

One night at the bowling alley lounge, I saw this beautiful girl with big brown eyes sitting at a table with her girlfriend. I couldn't help but stare at those eyes. When our eyes met, my heart would skip a beat. I couldn't hear the music playing anymore and was trying to concentrate on my lack of breathing. I finally got the nerve to ask her for a dance. She said no and I went back to my seat. Another guy asked her and she said no to him as well. I saw her looking at me again. So, I decided to ask her for a dance one last time. This time she said yes. I enjoyed her company for the rest of the night. At the end of the night I asked for her phone number. She said, "I don't have a phone but I'll call you in the morning." I thought this is where it ended for sure. The next day, while making breakfast, she called me. I was shocked and elated. We dated for fourteen months, and in 1978 I married the brown-eyed woman who stole my heart. The losing streak of the late-bloomer was over. She must have seen something humorous in my caveman-style personality.

Larry found love too. After high school he bumped into Martha Kelly (the F-bomb Queen). Once they realized how compatible they were, they got married.

"Henry, I think Martha tolerates me but mostly enjoys keeping me in line."

Once girls came into the picture, the Windsor Park Boys grew up quicker. From Catholic school to the days we were interested in girls, we've accumulated a boatload of memories. If I could get stuck in time, I'd like to go back to those times.

I remember time going by a lot slower during the fifties, sixties, and seventies. I can still picture us collecting bottles, playing cards at Cochise's house, playing pool in Elvis's cellar, driving around playing our eight-track tapes, catching tadpoles in the Trench, sitting at the Rocks having a fire, listening to the frogs talk to one another, and watching Little Z in his homemade boat towing a smiling Mad Mike in a tire tube around the Pawtuxet River on a lazy hot summer day.

Before we knew it, we were pursuing different interests and goals. Some went to college, some joined the military, some got jobs and married. I guess we had to grow up sometime. No more sitting around in the shade of a tree on someone's lawn in Windsor Park.

But now that we're older adults, I like to look back at the things we did as kids. The stories seem so comical. Hey, we were just kids, figuring out life for ourselves. We weren't bad kids. We weren't out to hurt anybody. We just lived and learned.

I now realize life as a kid wasn't that bad. When your body starts to give you the finger and you need a good laugh, visit, text, e-mail, Zoom, or phone your childhood friends. We might have to embrace our age when we get old, but it's our childhood memories that will keep us young forever. The memories of the place you grew up in, and the kids you grew up with.

For us, it was in Windsor Park that we share the memories with the Windsor Park Boys.

Good friends are like stars. You don't always see them, but you know they are always there. Keep them close and reminisce!

SO, WHAT DID WE LEARN GROWING UP?

EVERYONE HAS A FUNNY STORY

Story told by my brother TJ:

One night, Dad picked me and my buddies up after a Pop Warner football practice game. He stopped up the street from our house in front of the Falcon Club to drop everyone off because he wanted to stop in for a beer. Dad was taking our football gear out of his trunk when another friend of mine saw us standing there. From behind, he thought my father was one of his friends and ran up behind Dad, pantsing him. When Dad turned around, my friend's eyes bulged out of his head. I watched my father pulling up his pants and underwear, chasing him down the street and throwing his keys at him. It was priceless to see the whole thing go down. Dad really needed a drink that night.

———— ((•)) ————

This story was told to me by a patron who used to drink at the Falcon Club where my dad frequently stopped.

One snowy Friday night Dad and his best friend Jim were supposed to meet at the club. Jim never showed up so he called him. Jim lived just behind the club. He told my dad he was dying for a couple of beers but couldn't come over and had no beer at his house. His wife said he was drinking too much and told him he was going to sleep in the doghouse if he went over there.

The patron said it was snowing pretty hard that night, so my dad told Jim to go outside and shovel snow in about twenty minutes. Dad bought bottles of beer from the club and he and the patron drove by Jim's house, putting the beers in a snowbank next to his house. I can imagine Jim telling his wife he was going outside to shovel snow before it accumulated way too much. I can also imagine them laughing their heads off the next time they all got together.

———————

Story told by my Uncle Vinny:

In the 1960s Rhode Island was one of the most dangerous places in the nation at that time. Mob boss Raymond Patriarca Sr. made his headquarters there. He gained a reputation for fairness, but if crossed he could be the most ruthless of men. During that time, it was well known that a Rhode Island banker was skimming money from his bank and customers. One night while on our way to a Roaring-Twenties party, my friends and I stopped at a liquor store in North Smithfield, Rhode Island, to buy liquor, cigarettes, gum, etc. Lo and behold the banker was in there buying bottles of liquor. We were all decked out for the costume party in suits with ties and hats. We noticed the banker staring at us and getting really nervous. My friends and I didn't understand why he was sending us all this nervous tension, until another one of our friends came in carrying a violin case dressed like Al Capone. The banker almost dropped a biscuit in his pants. He thought someone paid the Mob to whack him. He dropped the bottles of liquor, smashing them on the floor, and ran out the door. We laughed all the way to the party.

———————

Two stories told by Rider:

As my father got really old his hearing started to go. One day when my family and I were at his house visiting, my kids watched my father mow his lawn with his gas mower, while I went to do an errand. When I came back my kids got me aside and said, "Grandpa pulled the cord to start the mower but it didn't start. He's been pushing the mower all around the house." When I approached my father, he said, "The mower isn't cutting too well." I had to tell him it's because it wasn't running.

Every Sunday my father would drive through town to get a cup of coffee, newspaper, and lottery ticket.

One cold Sunday morning he started up his car, revving his engine to warm it up. He didn't realize that his car gas accelerator got stuck under the floor mat after he revved the engine. He couldn't hear the engine screaming out of control. When he put the vehicle in reverse, the car shot out of the driveway and across the road. His door opened and it hit the neighbor's tree, then the rear of his car hit the corner of my neighbor's house. Realizing where he was, he put the vehicle in drive and it shot back across the road into our driveway. About a week before this, the neighbor behind my father's house had a large pile of loam dumped behind his house right on the property lines to fill uneven spots in his lawn. Dad buried his car into the pile, which stopped it from going into another neighbor's house. Dad realized it was time to give up his license.

As funny as it looked, we're all grateful that my father's pride was the only thing that got hurt.

—◦((◦))◦—

Story told by my father's neighbor Ed:

I decided to take out my golf clubs and started chipping balls on the side of my house. Things were going great until I miscalculated my strength and the ball shot over to TJ's father's house. His dad was sitting on his deck in his pajamas and bathrobe, trying to enjoy the fall day. I watched the golf ball ricochet off his roof, shoot down to his porch railing, and bounce around him like a pinball. I worried the ball hit him and rushed over. I told TJ's dad what I did and apologized. TJ's dad said he saw something white go by him but didn't know what it was. I looked for the ball but it seemed to have disappeared. TJ's dad happened to put his hand inside his bathrobe's pocket and found the ball. We laughed at a shot I never want to repeat.

———◦((◦))◦———

Story told by one of my doctors:

My dad went to visit his father at the nursing home. He wanted to bring him a gift and knew he loved chocolates. So, he stopped at the store and picked up a box of chocolates. My grandfather was ecstatic and started eating them. He told my dad the chocolates were very chewy. My dad decided to have one to see if in fact they were chewy. It wasn't until then that he realized something was wrong. He had bought the display box of chocolates that looked real but were made of silicone. Thank God silicone is not absorbed into the body. Dad's story circulates through all the family get-togethers. A story we'll all never let him live down.

What's your funny story?
I'd love to hear it: crazypaulri@gmail.com

Lightning Source UK Ltd.
Milton Keynes UK
UKHW020727090223
416597UK00011B/462

9 781977 254009